# Florence Parry Heide

# The **Bigness** Contest

## Illustrated by Victoria Chess

Little, Brown and Company

Boston   New York   Toronto   London

With love to my grandchildren,
whom I list in order of their appearance:
Heather, David, Dai, Win, Anne, Nora, and Donny
— F. P. H.

For Augie and Peter, with love
— V. C.

Text copyright © 1994 by Florence Parry Heide
Illustrations copyright © 1994 by Victoria Chess

First Edition

Library of Congress Cataloging-in-Publication Data

Heide, Florence Parry.
 The bigness contest / by Florence Parry Heide ; illustrated by
Victoria Chess. — 1st ed.
  p.  cm.
 Summary: A young hippopotamus worries that he is too big to be
good at anything, but with the help of Aunt Emerald, he learns that
"You can always find something to be good at. You just have to find
out what it is."
 ISBN 0-316-35444-9
 [1. Hippopotamus — Fiction.  2. Individuality — Fiction.]
I. Chess, Victoria, ill.  II. Title.
PZ7.H36Bi   1994
[E] — dc20                                              92-12663

10  9  8  7  6  5  4  3  2

SC

Published simultaneously in Canada
by Little, Brown & Company (Canada) Limited

Printed in Hong Kong

Beasley was very big.
And getting bigger every day.

"I'm much too big," he grumbled.

"Nonsense," said Aunt Emerald. "Hippopotamuses are supposed to be big."

Beasley sighed.

"I'm too big to be good at anything," he said. "And I want to be good at something. I want to win a blue ribbon. A big blue ribbon with gold letters that spell FIRST PRIZE."

There were plenty of contests.
Beasley had tried them all.

He had tried the Running Contest,
the High Jump Contest,
the Jump Rope Contest,
and the Somersault Contest. . . .

But he had never won.

He hadn't even won the Best Costume Contest.

Everything he had tried on was too small for him.

"I'm too big to win a contest," said Beasley sadly. "I'll never have a blue ribbon."

"Never give up," said Aunt Emerald. "You can always find *something* that you can do well. You don't know how good you can be at something until you try. That's what contests are for."

"I'm too big to be good at anything," said Beasley.

"Nonsense," said Aunt Emerald.

Beasley kept growing bigger and bigger and bigger.
He grew and he grew and he grew.

"Goodness gracious," said Aunt Emerald. "You *are* big, Beasley! You're the biggest hippopotamus I've ever seen. And I've seen many a hippopotamus in my day."

Beasley went down to the river to look at his reflection.

His cousin Borofil was sitting in the river.

Borofil was very lazy. Borofil never did anything.

Except sit in the water, of course. He was very good at that.

"Hey, Borofil," said Beasley, "look how big I am."

Borofil yawned.

"I'm the biggest hippopotamus Aunt Emerald has ever seen," said Beasley.

"So what?" said Borofil.

"Well, it would be something to be the biggest hippopotamus in the whole world," said Beasley. "I could win a blue ribbon. I've always wanted a blue ribbon."

He thought for a moment.

"I think I'll ask Aunt Emerald to have a Bigness Contest," he said. "That way I'd know for sure that I'm the biggest. It would be nice to be sure. And it would be nice to have a blue ribbon."

So Beasley asked Aunt Emerald if she would please
have a Bigness Contest.

Aunt Emerald thought it was a very good idea.

She put signs all around.

The signs said  BIGNESS CONTEST.

The next day, hippopotamuses started to come.

Buses and trains and boats and planes came, and all of them were packed with hippopotamuses.

Every single one of them wanted to win the contest.
Oh, dear, thought Beasley, they're pretty big.

Beasley had always hated being big.
Now he liked it.
Beasley had always tried to diet, to get thin.

Now he ate all the time, to get fat.
Banana splits, apple pies, ice cream cones, chocolate cakes with chocolate icing.
He ate and he ate and he ate.

He had always exercised, to get thin.
Now he just sat around, to get fat.
He sat and he sat and he sat.
He really worked at getting big.

The day of the contest came.

Aunt Emerald measured all of the hippopotamuses.

Not one of them was as long or as high or as round or as wide as Beasley.

So of course Beasley won.

He won a blue ribbon.

He put it around his neck. It looked very nice.

"Just what I've always wanted," said Beasley.

"Congratulations, Beasley," said Aunt Emerald.
"It's just what I've always said: you can always find
*something* to be good at."

Beasley went down to the river to look at his reflection. Borofil was still sitting in the water.

"Hey, Borofil, I won the Bigness Contest," said Beasley.

"So what?" asked Borofil.

"Well, now I have a blue ribbon," said Beasley.

"So what?" said Borofil, yawning.

"It means I was good at something," said Beasley.

"So?" said Borofil.

Borofil kept sitting in the water, and Beasley kept looking at his blue ribbon.

All the hippopotamuses came down to the river to have a bath.

There wasn't room for all of them.

"You've been in long enough, Borofil," said Aunt Emerald. "You'll have to get out until the rest of us have had a chance to get in."

"All right," sighed Borofil, "but I would like my same place back. It's so comfy."

Borofil slowly waddled out of the river.

"Goodness gracious, Borofil," said Aunt Emerald. "You're certainly BIG."

Borofil *was* big.

He was the biggest hippopotamus Aunt Emerald had ever seen.

He was bigger than Beasley.

"*You're* the biggest hippopotamus, Borofil," said Beasley. "Not me, after all. You."

Beasley gave Borofil his blue ribbon.

"Thank you," said Borofil. He put the blue ribbon around his own neck. It looked very nice.

"Now I'm only the second-biggest hippopotamus in the world," Beasley said sadly.

He kept looking at Borofil's blue ribbon while all the other hippopotamuses left.

Then Beasley climbed into the river and sat next to Borofil.

"I think I'll practice being lazy," he said. "I could get good at that."

So he practiced.

Day after day, Beasley sat in the river with Borofil.

Day after day after day, he sat and he sat and he sat.
He got to be very, very lazy.
He was too lazy to move.
He was too lazy to be bored.
He was too lazy to yawn.

"Goodness gracious," said Aunt Emerald. "You're getting to be very, very lazy, Beasley."

She thought for a moment.

"I think I'll have a Laziness Contest," she said.

And she did.

Beasley won. He won a blue ribbon, which is what he had always wanted.

"It proves what I've said all along," said Aunt Emerald. "You can always find *something* to be good at. You just have to try to find out what it is."

Now Beasley and Borofil sit together in the river with their blue ribbons around their necks.

They are very, very big.

They are very, very lazy.

They are very, very happy, but they are too lazy to smile.